Biddy and Dee Dee

PRAISE FOR *STORYSHARES*

"One of the brightest innovators and game-changers in the education industry."
– Forbes

"Your success in applying research-validated practices to promote literacy serves as a valuable model for other organizations seeking to create evidence-based literacy programs."

- Library of Congress

"We need powerful social and educational innovation, and Storyshares is breaking new ground. The organization addresses critical problems facing our students and teachers. I am excited about the strategies it brings to the collective work of making sure every student has an equal chance in life."
– Teach For America

"Around the world, this is one of the up-and-coming trailblazers changing the landscape of literacy and education."
- International Literacy Association

"It's the perfect idea. There's really nothing like this. I mean wow, this will be a wonderful experience for young people."   - Andrea Davis Pinkney, Executive Director, Scholastic

"Reading for meaning opens opportunities for a lifetime of learning. Providing emerging readers with engaging texts that are designed to offer both challenges and support for each individual will improve their lives for years to come. Storyshares is a wonderful start."
- David Rose, Co-founder of CAST & UDL

Biddy and Dee Dee

Elizabeth Player

STORYSHARES

New York. Boston. Philadelphia

Storyshares
Story Share, Inc.
24 N. Bryn Mawr Avenue #340
Bryn Mawr, PA 19010-3304
www.storyshares.org

Inspiring reading with a new kind of book.

Interest Level: High and Post High School
Grade Level Equivalent: 3.3

9781642619928

Book design by Storyshares

Storyshares Presents

1

It was love at first sight.

When Henry bent to stroke the excitable pup, she jumped, licked, squeaked, and rolled onto her back. With her shiny black coat and clear white markings on her chest and ears, she was irresistible.

The girl from the shelter said, "She came in two days ago. The farmer from over Wolston way said he found her worrying sheep. She's lucky she wasn't shot."

I'd been toying with the idea of a dog for a while, trying to decide if it was a good idea or not. Watching

Henry's reaction to the adorable pup was the only confirmation I needed.

I was glad we had come to the shelter.

I asked, "So you have no idea where she came from?"

The girl shook her head. "No collar. The only thing I can tell you is that she's been well cared for. We guess she's around five months old. And she looks like she's a collie...and some other breed.

"We wait one week to give an owner the chance to turn up. If they don't show, we can then begin the adoption process."

Henry blurted out, "I'm nearly five, and I'm a big boy now, Mummy! Look, she loves me. Can she be our pet... please?"

My heart melted. My boy rarely demonstrated such an outpouring of delight and affection—for anything.

I smiled. "Well, if nobody comes to claim her, I don't see why not."

He leapt to his feet and gave a loud "yippee!" then ran up and down the shelter aisle. The pup ran with him, nipping at his sleeve.

2

The following week dragged by. If Henry asked once, he asked a thousand times a day, "When is she coming Mummy? Can I call her Biddy, like the naughty dog in my storybook?"

It was difficult to make him understand why we had to wait.

Finally, seven days had passed, and I made the call.

I held my breath when the receptionist said she'd check on the status of the collie pup. "Yes! We still have her."

Now it was my turn to yell "yippee" and run up and down the hallway.

As Biddy settled into our home, the change in Henry was dramatic.

He'd recently been diagnosed with autism, though I'd known it in my gut for a long time.

He lived in his own little world. He had a hard time communicating his thoughts and feelings. He found new situations to be a real challenge.

I didn't know if Biddy also sensed his condition, but it was clear they were a match made in heaven.

Henry became part of Biddy's daily routine. He would feed her, walk her, and even brush her.

I couldn't get over how much his attention span had improved.

But then our happy bubble burst quickly and completely one Tuesday morning when the shelter manager called me. What she said left me shocked.

Biddy and Dee Dee

3

I heard the first sentence clearly, but then the words became jumbled. I couldn't really hear or understand what she was saying any more. My head spun and my chest ached.

I wrote down the number the manager gave me. Then sat at the kitchen table and cried like I hadn't cried for years.

Biddy ran to my side and whined. I bent down, and she nuzzled my neck. It was comforting. She even licked the tears off my cheeks.

I was grateful Henry was at pre-school.

A man who said he was Biddy's real owner had shown up at the shelter. He said he had been in the hospital in a coma, unconscious because he had been injured so badly.

That's why he hadn't come to get Biddy.

I was shocked. All I could think was *Really?!*

It felt like I was living a nightmare. What would I tell Henry?

I stared at the man's name and phone number forever. Finally, I made the call.

4

I sat in the back garden holding a newspaper. I hadn't even read it.

My stomach was in knots. When the doorbell rang, my heart started to pound.

Henry ran from the bottom of the garden with Biddy chasing behind. He shouted, "Who's that Mummy?"

"You stay here with Biddy. I'll go and see," I said.

I opened the front door. The man standing before me smiled awkwardly.

"Hello," he said. "I'm Christian Brassington."

We shook hands.

"I'm Moira. Pleased to meet you," I said, but it was a lie.

When Biddy saw the visitor, she went crazy. With some difficulty, the man stooped down, geting close to her level.

She jumped all over him. She was crying and licking his face. It was obvious this man was not a stranger to her.

I was heartbroken as I stood there, watching their touching little reunion.

The knife in my heart received one final twist when the man said, "Hello Dee Dee! I've missed you, girl."

He let her nuzzle into his neck.

"She obviously knows you." My voice shook.

Henry came up behind me and pulled at my sweater. "She's not Dee Dee. She's Biddy."

To reassure him, I said, "This is Mr. Brassington, and he's come to pay us all a visit."

Henry looked confused for a moment, but then he ran off with the pup chasing behind.

5

I invited the visitor to sit in the garden while I made us coffee. Waiting for the coffee to brew gave me time to think about the situation and the man.

Mr. Brassington was kind, friendly—very charming. But I was determined to keep Biddy for Henry.

I knew we were in an impossible situation. There was no easy answer. Someone would get hurt.

I didn't want it to be my son.

Through my open kitchen window, I could hear Henry chatting away with our visitor.

Henry told him how Biddy liked to lick his spoon when he had pudding. This made Mr. Brassington burst out laughing.

That was a first. Henry rarely talked to complete strangers.

I joined them in the garden and poured the coffee, I was aware of our visitor looking at me warily, not sure who I was or what I would want.

I said, "Would you prefer that I call you Mr Brassington or...?"

He gave a crooked smile and shook his head, "Christian, please. I still think the only Mr. Brassington is my dad."

We both smiled, but we were tense, uncomfortable.

He sat with one leg stretched out before him. He sipped his coffee, then briefly closed his eyes. He was enjoying the warmth of the sun on his face.

A light breeze lifted the curly brown hair from his forehead.

There was a raw-looking, red scar under his hair. It went from below his hair line, down his left temple, and along the side of his face.

I realized I felt a little bad for him. It made it easier to ask what had happened to him. Why had he been in a coma?

Biddy and Dee Dee

6

He straightened up, cleared his throat, and began his story.

"I was in an accident on the highway about six weeks ago. I swerved to avoid a goose. Damn thing flew right at me. I ended up wrapped around a tree in a ditch."

"My God! I'm so sorry," I said.

He nodded, and pointed to the scar on his face. "Perhaps if I'd stuck to the speed limit, things might have been different."

Try as I might, I couldn't find a lie in his story. "Do you mind telling me about your injuries?"

"Not at all. Cracked knee, broken ribs, and severe knock to the head.

The hatchback flew up on impact. Dee Dee was in her cage, but it opened, and she ran for her life. I spent three weeks in a coma and had a bit of memory loss, initially.

"I was moving because of a break-up. When my folks came to see me in the hospital, they assumed Dee Dee was staying with my ex. No one knew to look for her."

I made a real effort to keep my voice steady. "It's been six weeks Mr...err...Christian," I said.

I took a deep breath. "Are you here... to take Biddy away?"

He shifted uncomfortably in his chair and shook his head. "Of course not. You adopted her fair and square. I can see that she's fit in so well with your family."

His eyes looked beyond sad. I knew that he was hoping against hope I would disagree.

Biddy and Dee Dee

7

After a pause, I said, "It's not just Biddy, you see... it's my boy, Henry. He's autistic, and since she arrived... our lives... his life... has changed beyond measure."

His jaw dropped. He looked like he'd been punched in the stomach, very hard.

We sat in silence for a long while. Finally, he cleared his throat.

He complimented me on my excellent coffee and stayed for a second cup. We chatted about our work.

He was in construction. He had even been part of renovating an old church in our town a couple of years before.

He politely asked about my work as a self-employed pastry chef. He appeared genuinely impressed that I baked cupcakes and wedding cakes from home.

We continued on with our polite chit-chat, but my mind was elsewhere. I needed to get to the heart of why we were both sitting in my garden. He must have been thinking exactly the same thing.

"Look Moira," he spoke first. "I didn't come here to snatch Dee... *Biddy* away. I knew it wouldn't be straightforward.

"It looks like your need is greater than mine." His voice cracked, and his expression was pained.

I wanted to throw my arms about his neck.

Biddy and Henry ran back to the table. Christian Brassington was able to fuss over the dog, scratching her and giving her lots of love, before he turned to leave.

He shook hands with Henry and told him to take good care of Biddy... she was a very special dog.

Biddy and Dee Dee

8

When we reached the garden gate, Christian turned to me and said, "I see there's a street fair in the town next Saturday. They're having a dog show. Do you think Biddy might do well?"

I laughed. "If they have a 'best dog in the world' category, she'll win it, hands down."

A crooked smile lit up his face.

"Why don't we all go together?" I suggested.

He nodded enthusiastically. "That's a date, then, Moira. I'll see you, Henry, and Biddy at the fair next Saturday!"

I watched him go. If a limping man could have a spring in his step, then Christian absolutely did.

Biddy and Henry spilled onto the front lawn a moment later. For a brief second, they were quiet. They were both watching as Christian drove away.

"Mummy, is that man our friend?" Henry asked. "Biddy really liked him."

"Yes," I told him, "I think we'll all become very good friends indeed."

About The Author

Elizabeth Player is a semi-retired teacher, now writer, living in the glorious county of Cornwall where walking along the many coastal paths provides great thinking time for her next story.

Biddy and Dee Dee

About The Publisher

Storyshares is a nonprofit focused on supporting the millions of teens and adults who struggle with reading by creating a new shelf in the library specifically for them. The ever-growing collection features content that is compelling and culturally relevant for teens and adults, yet still readable at a range of lower reading levels.

Storyshares generates content by engaging deeply with writers, bringing together a community to create this new kind of book. With more intriguing and approachable stories to choose from, the teens and adults who have fallen behind are improving their skills and beginning to discover the joy of reading. For more information, visit storyshares.org.

Easy to Read. Hard to Put Down.

Biddy and Dee Dee

www.ingramcontent.com/pod-product-compliance
Lightning Source LLC
Chambersburg PA
CBHW071229170626
46809CB00005BA/1993